ZOG

By Julia Donaldson

Illustrated by Axel Scheffler

Madam Dragon ran a school, many moons ago.
She taught young dragons all the things that dragons need to know.

Zog, the biggest dragon, was the keenest one by far.
He tried his hardest every day to win a golden star.

All the dragons in Year One were learning how to fly.
"High!" said Madam Dragon. "Way up in the sky!

"Now that you've been shown, you can practise on your own
And you'll all be expert fliers by the time you're fully grown."

Zog went off to practise,
flying fast and free.

He soared and swooped
and looped the loop . . .

then crashed into a tree.

Just then, a little girl came by. "Oh, please don't cry," she said.
"Perhaps you'd like a nice sticky plaster for your head?"

"What a good idea!" said Zog. Then up and off he flew,
His plaster gleaming pinkly as he zigzagged through the blue.

A year went by, and in Year Two the dragons learned to roar.
"More!" said Madam Dragon. "Louder, I implore!
Now that you've been shown, you can practise on your own
And you'll all be champion roarers by the time you're fully grown."

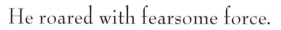

Zog went off to practise.

He roared with fearsome force.

He kept it up for hours on end . . .

but then his throat grew hoarse.

Just then the girl came by again. She said, "What rotten luck!
Perhaps you'd like a nice soothing peppermint to suck?"

"What a good idea!" said Zog. Then up and off he flew,
And breathing fumes of peppermint he zigzagged through the blue.

A year went by, and in Year Three the dragons learned to blow.

"No!" said Madam Dragon. "Breathe out fire, not snow!

Now that you've been shown, you can practise on your own

And you'll all be breathing bonfires by the time you're fully grown."

Zog went off to practise.

He blew with all his might.

He twirled around in triumph . . .

and his wing tip caught alight.

Just then the girl came by again. She said, "You poor old thing. Perhaps you'd like a nice stretchy bandage for your wing?"

"What a good idea!" said Zog. Then up and off he flew,
His bandage flapping wildly as he zigzagged through the blue.

All the Year Four dragons were learning — can you guess?
"Yes!" said Madam Dragon. "How to capture a princess!

"Now that you've been shown, you can practise on your own.
You'll need to capture hundreds by the time you're fully grown."

Zog went off to practise.
    He tried and tried and tried,
But he simply couldn't manage.
    "I'm no good at this," he cried.

"I'll *never* win a golden star!"
    Just then he saw the girl.
"Perhaps," she said, "you'd like to capture *me*?
    I'm Princess Pearl."

"What a good idea!" said Zog.
    Then up and off they flew,
The princess gripping tightly
    as they zigzagged through the blue.

"Ah," said Madam Dragon. "Our first princess so far!
Congratulations, Zog, my dear; you've won a golden star!"

Zog was proud and happy,
and Pearl felt good as well.

She took the dragons' temperatures,

and nursed them when they fell.

Zog breathed fire and beat his wings. "You can't! She's mine!" he roared.
"Oh, no, she's not!" yelled Gadabout, and waved his trusty sword.

The other dragons crowded round and watched them, all agog.
Who was going to win the fight, Sir Gadabout or Zog?

Then Zog said, "Flying doctors! I'd love to join the crew.
If you'll let me be your ambulance, then I can carry you."
"Bravo!" said Madam Dragon. "An excellent career!"
And all the Year Five dragons gave a loud resounding cheer.

Then Madam Dragon told the horse, "I really hope you'll stay.
I'll let you be my pupils' pet, and feed you lots of hay."

"What a good idea!" said Zog. Then up and off he flew,
The Flying Doctors waving as they zigzagged through the blue.

For Poppy – J.D.
For Gabriel and Raphael – A.S.

First published in the UK in 2010 by
Alison Green Books
An imprint of Scholastic Children's Books
Euston House, 24 Eversholt Street
London NW1 1DB, UK
A division of Scholastic Ltd
www.scholastic.co.uk
London – New York – Toronto – Sydney – Auckland
Mexico City – New Delhi – Hong Kong

Text copyright © 2010 Julia Donaldson
Illustrations copyright © 2010 Axel Scheffler

HB ISBN: 978 1 407115 56 6

9 10 8

The moral rights of Julia Donaldson and Axel Scheffler have been asserted.

Papers used by Scholastic Children's Books are made from wood grown in sustainable forests.